Dear Parent:

Congratulations! Your child is taking the first steps on an exciting journey. The destination? Independent reading!

STEP INTO READING® will help your child get there. The program offers five steps to reading success. Each step includes fun stories and colorful art. There are also Step into Reading Sticker Books, Step into Reading Math Readers, Step into Reading Write-In Readers, Step into Reading Phonics Readers, and Step into Reading Phonics First Steps! Boxed Sets—a complete literacy program with something for every child.

Learning to Read, Step by Step!

Ready to Read   Preschool–Kindergarten
• big type and easy words • rhyme and rhythm • picture clues
For children who know the alphabet and are eager to begin reading.

Reading with Help   Preschool–Grade 1
• basic vocabulary • short sentences • simple stories
For children who recognize familiar words and sound out new words with help.

Reading on Your Own   Grades 1–3
• engaging characters • easy-to-follow plots • popular topics
For children who are ready to read on their own.

Reading Paragraphs   Grades 2–3
• challenging vocabulary • short paragraphs • exciting stories
For newly independent readers who read simple sentences with confidence.

Ready for Chapters   Grades 2–4
• chapters • longer paragraphs • full-color art
For children who want to take the plunge into chapter books but still like colorful pictures.

STEP INTO READING® is designed to give every child a successful reading experience. The grade levels are only guides. Children can progress through the steps at their own speed, developing confidence in their reading, no matter what their grade.

Remember, a lifetime love of reading starts with a single step!

To Seamus

www.stepintoreading.com

www.randomhouse.com/kids/disney

Educators and librarians, for a variety of teaching tools, visit us at www.randomhouse.com/teachers

Library of Congress Cataloging-in-Publication Data
Richards, Kitty.
  Run, Remy, Run! / by Kitty Richards; illustrated by the Disney Storybook Artists.
      p. cm. — (Step into reading. A step 1 book)
ISBN: 978-0-7364-2476-9 (trade)
ISBN: 978-0-7364-8054-3 (lib. bdg.)
I. Disney Storybook Artists. II. Ratatouille (Motion picture) III. Title. PZ7.R387Run 2007
2006037142

Printed in the United States of America   10 9 8 7 6 5 4 3 2 1   First Edition

STEP INTO READING, RANDOM HOUSE, and the Random House colophon are registered trademarks of Random House, Inc.

STEP INTO READING®

STEP 1

Disney·PIXAR

RATATOUILLE
(rat·a·too·ee)

Run, Remy, Run!

By Kitty Richards

Illustrated by the Disney Storybook Artists

Random House 🏠 New York

This is Remy.

Remy is not like
the other rats.

He walks on two feet.

He reads books.

He watches TV.

He wants to be a chef!

One day, Remy gets lost.
He ends up in Paris.

Remy watches a boy
make soup.

The boy spills the soup.
What will he do?

10

The boy makes more soup.

But the soup is bad!

The skylight opens!

Remy falls down!

Remy lands in the sink.

Swim, Remy, swim!

Remy gets out.
But he is scared.

The kitchen is busy.

Run, Remy, run!

Remy sees

an open window.

Will he get out?

Climb, Remy, climb!

Oh, no!

Remy falls into a pot.

Jump, Remy, jump!

He lands in a pan!

Jump, Remy, jump!

Remy sees the boy.

The boy tastes the soup.
Yuck!

Run, Remy, run!

But Remy stops running.

He smells the soup.

The soup stinks!

Remy wants to fix it.

Cook, Remy, cook!

Uh-oh!

The boy sees Remy.

The chef sees the boy.

He is angry.

No one is watching.

The soup gets served!

Will the soup
taste good?

Yes!

That rat can cook!